WE'RE GOING ON A LION HUNT

Adapted by
Margery Cuyler

Illustrated by
Joe Mathieu

SCHOLASTIC INC.
New York Toronto London Auckland
Sydney Mexico City New Delhi Hong Kong

ISBN 978-0-545-34556-9

Text copyright © 2008 by Margery Cuyler.
Illustrations copyright © 2008 by Joe Mathieu. All rights reserved.
Published by Scholastic Inc., 557 Broadway, New York, NY 10012,
by arrangement with Marshall Cavendish Corporation. SCHOLASTIC
and associated logos are trademarks and/or registered trademarks
of Scholastic Inc.

12 11 10 9 8 7 6 5 4 3 2 1   11 12 13 14 15 16/0

Printed in the U.S.A.   08

This edition first printing, January 2011

The artwork was rendered with Prismacolor pencils
and Luna watercolors on Lanaquarelle paper.
Book design by Vera Soki

For Juliana and Dick Fenn
—M.C.

To my beautiful granddaughter, Bella
—J.M.

Get ready! We're going on a lion hunt. Time to put on your safari hats. Time to use your imagination.

Aa Bb Cc Dd Ee Ff Gg

We're going on a lion hunt.
We're going to catch a big one.

We're not afraid.
Look what's up ahead!

Mud!
Can't go over it.
Can't go under it.

Can't go around it.
Have to go through it.
Slog, slog, slog.

We're going on a lion hunt.
We're going to catch a big one.
We're not afraid.
Look what's up ahead!

Sticks!
Can't go over them.
Can't go under them.
Can't go around them.
Have to go through them.
Snap, snap, snap.

We're going on a lion hunt.
We're going to catch a big one.
We're not afraid.
Look what's up ahead!

Trees!
Can't go over them.
Can't go under them.
Can't go around them.
Have to climb up them.
Up we go, up we go, up we go.

We're going on a lion hunt.
We're going to catch a big one.
We're not afraid.
Look what's up ahead!
River!

Can't go over it.
Can't go under it.
Can't go around it.
Have to go through it.
Splish-splash, splish-splash, splish-splash.

We're going on a lion hunt.
We're going to catch a big one.
We're not afraid.
Look what's up ahead!
Grass!

Can't go over it.
Can't go under it.
Can't go around it.
Have to go through it.
Swish, swish, swish.

We're going on a lion hunt.
We're going to catch a big one.
We're not afraid.
Look what's up ahead!
Cave!

Can't go over it.
Can't go under it.
Can't go around it.
Have to go through it.
We're not afraid.

OOOo-oooO.

It's dark in here.
We see two shining lights.
We feel something furry.
We feel a c-c-c-cold nose.
We feel s-s-s-sharp teeth.

It's a lion!
Run out of the cave.

Crawl through the grass.

Swim across the river.

Climb up the trees.

Jump through the sticks.

Slosh through the mud.

Run into the school.
Close the door.

Safe at last!